PERCEVAL

KING ARTHUR'S KNIGHT
OF THE HOLY GRAIL

RETOLD BY

JOHN PERKINS

FROM CHRÉTIEN DE TROYES

ILLUSTRATED BY

GENNADY SPIRIN

MARSHALL CAVENDISH CHILDREN

Marshall Cavendish Corporation, 99 White Plains Road, Tarrytown, New York 10591
www.marshallcavendish.us

LIBRARY OF CONGRESS CATALOGING-IN-PUBLICATION DATA
Perkins, John.
Perceval : King Arthur's Knight of the Holy Grail / retold by John Perkins from Chrétien de Troyes ;
illustrated by Gennady Spirin. — 1st ed.
p. cm.
Summary: Retells the Arthurian legend of Perceval, a foolish and impatient boy
who realizes his dream of becoming a great knight, but meets with
misfortune when he forgets to pray and serve God.
ISBN-13: 978-0-7614-5339-0
1. Perceval (Legendary character)—Legends. [1. Perceval (Legendary character)—Legends.
2. Knights and knighthood—Folklore. 3. Christian life—Folklore. 4. Folklore—England.]
I. Chrétien, de Troyes, 12th cent. II. Spirin, Gennadii, ill. III. Title.
PZ8.1.P415Per 2007
398.2—dc22
2006013118

The text of this book is set in ost Medieval.
The illustrations were rendered in egg tempura.

Book design by Michael Nelson

Printed in China
First edition
1 3 5 6 4 2

Marshall Cavendish
Children

One spring morning, when the birds began the new day with their bright singing, a young boy left his mother's house in the Desolate Forest. With a glad heart he saddled his old mare and took along three javelins for hunting. After riding some distance, he set his horse to graze near the field where his mother's plowmen were sowing oats. Then, clutching his small spears, he entered the forest.

As he was flinging his javelins, he heard the clanging and jingling sounds of armor. Then he saw five knights in shining helmets, dressed in

colors as bright as a rainbow, riding through the forest. The youth thought, "These must be God and his angels whom my mother told me I should worship!" Immediately he threw himself to the ground and prayed.

The leader of the knights rode up and said gently, "Do not be afraid."

"I am not afraid," said the boy. "But are you God?"

"No, foolish boy, I swear I am a knight!"

"I have never seen a knight before," exclaimed the boy. "You are more beautiful than God! I wish I were a knight, glittering and strong. Were you born wearing this gleaming metal?"

"My companions and I were given our armor and rank at King Arthur's court. We departed from there only five days ago."

"Tell me more about this king who makes knights, and where he can be found," the boy pleaded.

"He is at Carlisle, if he hasn't moved on. But tell me, what is your name, my boy?"

"My name is Darling Son."

"But don't you have a real name?"

"Darling Brother."

"I mean your proper name."

"Darling Little Lord."

Hearing this, the knight chuckled. "What a rare wonder we have here!" Then he turned his horse and galloped away with his companions.

The boy hurried home, eager to tell his mother about his meeting with the knights.

His mother was sick with worry that he had been gone so long. "Darling son," she asked, "where have you been all this time?"

"Mother, I have seen creatures even more beautiful than God and his angels! They are called knights! They come from King Arthur's court. I want to be a knight, too. I will go now in search of King Arthur!"

At this, his mother collapsed from shock. Then, recovering her senses, she explained to her son, "Alas, I had hoped to protect you from the world of knighthood and chivalry. Your father and your brothers were knights of the highest honor, feared and dreaded in all these lands. I, myself, am descended from knights and ladies. But once during a battle your father was wounded in his thigh and became crippled. His lands went to ruin and he became as poor as a beggar. Your two brothers were killed in knightly combat. Your father finally died of grief at their loss. God has left you alone with me as my only joy and happiness."

But the impatient youth cared not a turnip for any of this. "I must go now to King Arthur's court and meet the one who makes knights," he insisted.

His mother tried to discourage him, but it was like talking to a stump. At last, she yielded and gave him a homespun Welsh suit: a canvas shirt, breeches and leggings, and a hooded deerskin coat. When her son was ready to leave, his mother advised him, "Honor all ladies and aid those in distress. If earned, you may accept the reward of a kiss or a ring or a coin from a lady's purse, but nothing more. Always learn the name of a companion with whom you travel or lodge for any length of time and go with worthy men, seeking their advice. Visit God's house, our Holy Church, and pray often to Our Lord that He grant you joy and honor."

At the bridge, the boy's mother tearfully kissed him good-bye, praying that God would keep him safe. Lingering no longer, the boy urged his horse forward. After he rode a short distance, he glanced back and saw that his mother had collapsed on the ground, lying as still as a log. Nevertheless, he spurred his horse forward, bounding full speed into the dark forest. He rode straight ahead, and at night-fall he slept beneath the trees till the morning sun appeared like a glittering ruby in the east.

heered by the brilliant forest song, the boy mounted his horse and rode until he reached an open field, where the green grass was as lush and soft as velvet. Here, by a spring, he saw a scarlet-and-gold pavilion sparkling in the sun's glare. "This is God's house!" thought the boy. "I must enter here and worship Him as my mother told me. I will pray for food!" Barging in on his horse, he saw a girl sleeping on a bed covered with rich silk brocade. The maiden suddenly

awoke, startled by this clumsy fool who declared, "My mother told me to greet young ladies with a kiss."

The girl replied, "You had better get away from here, for if my lover finds you, he will kill you!"

The boy ignored her warning and leaped at her, kissing her twenty times without stopping. Then he noticed a dazzling emerald ring on the maiden's finger. "My mother told me I should take your ring," he said.

"I shall certainly not give it to you!" she cried.

But the boy grabbed her hand and forced the ring from her finger, shouting, "Thank you, dear lady! I wish all God's blessings on you."

After helping himself to some venison pies and wine, the youth swung himself onto his horse and rode away, leaving the damsel wailing at her dreadful plight.

ater that day the boy met a charcoal-burner who gave him directions to Carlisle. The boy rode toward the sea, where he came to a magnificent fortified castle. Its walls were thick and high, pierced by hundreds of narrow windows. Pennants streamed from the ramparts like brilliantly colored ribbons. As the youth drew near, he spied a knight dressed all in red riding toward him over the drawbridge. The horseman carried a fine-looking gold cup. Admiring the knight's red armor, the boy thought, "I would like that armor for myself! I shall ask the king for it."

As they passed each other on the open field before the drawbridge, the Red Knight shouted, "Where are you going, my lad?"

The boy replied boldly, "I am on my way to King Arthur's court, where I will ask for your crimson armor, that I may wear it as my very own."

"Well enough," said the Red Knight. "Go in and tell your King Arthur to surrender his castle to me or else put up a fair fight. I make claim to all this land, and I shall certainly have it as my own! Look here! A moment ago I took this precious cup, still full of wine, from the king's hand as proof that this land is mine."

The boy had no intention of delivering this message to the king, since he didn't understand one bit of it. Riding directly into the castle, he barged into the great hall.

King Arthur was seated silently at the head table, lost in thought. The boy rode closer and greeted him, but there was no answer. "This king does not say a word. How can he create knights?" wondered the boy. Then the foolish lad rode closer, and his horse knocked off the king's gold crown. Arthur awoke from his trance and greeted the boy, explaining, "I did not speak to you sooner because of my burning anger at a knight who recently threatened to take my lands. He is called the Red Knight from the Forest of Quinqueroi. He seized my cup so arrogantly that he spilled wine all over the queen! She has departed to her rooms."

The boy cared not an onion for any of this. He simply declared, "Make me a knight, my good king, for I wish to be on my way!" As the boy spoke, his eyes flashed with impatience. The rest of the hall was filled with members of the royal court who watched the youth, thinking him handsome and brave, but also quite foolish.

7

"For your good and mine, I will indeed make you a knight," proclaimed the king. "But first you must dismount and hand over your horse to my squire Yonet for safe-keeping."

"The man I met outside never dismounted," retorted the boy, "so why should I? Make me a knight now so that I may be off!"

"In truth you're a curious fellow," replied the king. "But for your benefit and my honor, I will grant you your wish."

"By my faith in God, I will not be a knight unless I can be a red knight! Give me the armor of the man who stole your cup!"

Sir Kay, a knight who possessed a sharp tongue, exclaimed, "Certainly you were no fool to come here and seek the Red Knight's armor. They are yours indeed!" But he was just making fun of the silly child.

"Sir Kay," replied Arthur, "you are too quick to insult the boy. Your scornful words ill-befit your knightly station. Despite being foolish, the lad seems to be of noble descent."

As the youth turned to leave, he caught sight of a striking young lady seated among the royal company. As he greeted her, a look of joy rose into her eyes and she began to laugh. Bursting with delight, she proclaimed before the entire assembly, "Young man, I think that if you live, there never was, nor will there ever be, a greater knight than you in all the world. This I know to be God's own truth!" In the hush that followed, all were astonished, because the lady had not laughed in more than six years.

Sir Kay, who had a bad temper, suddenly struck the maiden so hard that she fell to the floor. Then he kicked the court fool into the hearth fire, because the fool had so often declared, "Yonder maiden shall never laugh again until she beholds the one who will be the greatest master of chivalry that ever lived."

The youth, his mind set on one thing only, rode out of the castle at full gallop and sped after the Red Knight.

he squire Yonet promptly followed the youth into the field, where the Red Knight was waiting. The boy hurried toward the knight. "Lay down your armor as King Arthur has ordered!" he exclaimed.

"Has the king sent no one brave enough to fight for him?" teased the knight.

"I say, lay down your armor at once or I shall attack you!" replied the youth. At this, the Red Knight swung the blunt end of his lance at the youth's shoulders, slamming the boy forward in his saddle. In an instant the youth recovered, pulled a javelin from his belt, and shot it swiftly toward the

knight. The sharp dart pierced the knight's eye and drove deeply into his skull. Reeling, he toppled to the ground, his lifeless body sprawled upon the turf.

The youth dismounted, lay the Red Knight's lance to one side, and removed his red shield. But he had trouble lifting the helmet, because he had not been taught how to hold it properly. And he did not know how to unbuckle the sword or take it out of its scabbard. He yanked at the shirt of chain mail without success. Finally Yonet showed the eager boy how to remove the armor and clothing from the knight's body. Then Yonet advised the boy to dress himself in the knight's padded silk tunic before he put on the red armor. But the boy, sneering at the fine clothes, stubbornly preferred his own homespun canvas clothing and the rawhide boots that his mother had made. So he put the red armor on over his Welsh country suit. Resigned to the boy's wishes, Yonet adjusted each piece of armor and helped him mount the knight's horse. Then he showed the youth how to hold the lance and the shield. Before they parted company, the new Red Knight handed the king's gold cup to Yonet and gave him the old mare he no longer needed. "Please tell the maiden whom Kay struck that if I do live, I will avenge her honor." Yonet promised to deliver the message.

Then they departed, the youth to his next adventure and Yonet to the king. Yonet worried about the safety of the foolish boy who had no knowledge of knightly combat.

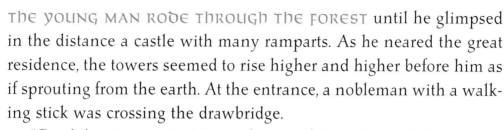

THE YOUNG MAN RODE THROUGH THE FOREST until he glimpsed in the distance a castle with many ramparts. As he neared the great residence, the towers seemed to rise higher and higher before him as if sprouting from the earth. At the entrance, a nobleman with a walking stick was crossing the drawbridge.

"Good day to you, sir. My mother taught me always to be courteous," called the boy.

"God bless you, friend. From whence do you come?"

"From King Arthur's court," replied the youth, "where he made me a knight!"

The worthy man questioned the boy carefully, until he had heard the story of the youth's life. He thought that the young man, though high born and well equipped, was quite foolish and knew next to nothing about knighthood. So he offered to teach the boy the rules of knightly combat and courtly manners.

The boy agreed. "My mother told me to go to worthy men for advice."

"Your mother, bless her, gave you good advice," replied the nobleman.

That very day the nobleman taught the youth the first lesson of knightly combat: desire, effort, and training are the source of all wisdom.

The boy worked hard at his lessons, but he asked many foolish questions and spoke often of his dear mother. As they entered the castle for the night, he said to his host, "My mother told me that I should inquire about the identity of any man with whom I travel or lodge. I would like to know your name, dear sir."

"Young man, my name is Gornemant of Gohort," the gentleman answered.

Gornemant invited the youth to stay until his training was complete. But the boy insisted that he leave the very next day, to discover the condition of his dear mother whom he had last seen collapsing from grief at the bridge.

That evening they enjoyed a sumptuous dinner, and then a servant led the youth to a well-appointed bedchamber for the night. In the morning, Gornemant brought him a present: a new suit of clothes, including a proper gentleman's blouse, knightly breeches, stockings, and a tunic of Indian silk. He advised the boy to discard his mother's rustic outfit, put on these new garments, and wear his chain-mail armor on the outside. Once again the boy argued that no clothes could be better than his mother's own handiwork, but in the end he followed the worthy man's advice.

"I have taught you only the basics of what you need to know about knighthood," Gornemant remarked. "I would add these last five points of advice:

"First, never slay an unarmed knight who begs for mercy.

"Second, don't ask so many questions, since you will be thought ignorant and foolish. Learn to control your silly curiosity and conduct yourself so that people will think you are a shrewd and experienced man.

"Third, if you encounter any woman in distress, assist her and offer her your protection.

"Fourth, go to the cathedral to pray to your heavenly Father, that He may have mercy upon you and protect you."

The boy blurted, "My mother gave me exactly this same advice!"

"Indeed! Just now we come to my final piece of advice," said Gornemant. "From now on, don't say it was your mother who taught you, or people will think that you are a foolish child, rather than a mature gentleman knight."

On the following day, with Gornemant's blessing and a prayer to God, the youth rode deep into the lonely forest, hoping to learn some news regarding his dear mother.

AFTER RIDING SOME DISTANCE, the boy came to the fortified town of Beaurepaire which was by a river flowing into the sea. The town's gates were locked, and after banging loudly, the boy saw a thin, pale maiden appear at an upper window. She called down, "What is it that you want, lad?"

He replied, "I need a place to lay my head."

After a long wait, four guards armed with axes and swords opened the gates.

As the boy entered the town, he saw only a few old, gaunt people. The buildings were as decrepit as the stones in an old graveyard. Dogs prowled the empty street, looking starved and sickly.

The youth was led into a slate-roofed castle and then into a great hall, where two elderly noblemen and a beautiful maiden greeted him.

he young lady, who took him by the hand, was finer looking than any exotic bird. She wore a raven-colored gown under a cloak of spotted fur that was lined in ermine. Her long, golden hair glowed as it spilled over her black-and-white sable collar. Her forehead was high and clear like a statue sculpted from softest ivory, and her brown eyebrows rose above laughing gray eyes that were set wide apart. Her nose was straight and long, and a lovely hue of crimson tinted the white skin of her cheeks. Still holding the boy's hand, the courteous lady seated herself on a couch spread with a coverlet woven of silk and gold thread. The youth took his place beside her as groups of knights entered the great hall and surrounded the couple, watching the handsome pair in silence.

For a long time the youth said nothing, remembering the advice of Gornemant. Finally the maiden asked him, "From whence did you ride this past day?"

I have just been the guest of a fine nobleman in a strong and magnificent castle. His name is Gornemant of Gohort."

The lady explained that Gornemant was her uncle. Her own name was Blanche Fleur, which meant "white flower." The maiden offered the youth a simple meal of six small loaves of bread from a nearby monastery, a small keg of mulled wine, and a little fresh, roasted deer. After they had eaten, a couch was made up in the hall for the youth, and Blanche Fleur wished him a pleasant rest. Then she retired to her own private chamber.

In the early hours of darkness the boy suddenly awoke, his face wet, and saw Blanche Fleur bending over him. Tears were spilling down her cheeks and onto his own. "Oh, dear friend," he said, "what is the trouble? Why do you weep so? Please tell me."

"I am the most miserable creature alive!" sobbed Blanche Fleur. "The cruel knight, Anguiguerron, steward of Prince Clamadeu of the Isles, has killed or imprisoned two hundred and sixty of our best fighting men. They will all die because of me. Anguiguerron seeks to take my lands and hold me hostage for Prince Clamadeu. Soon he will invade this weakened city and seize us by force. But if Clamadeu captures me he will never have my life or my soul, for I will kill myself before I shall submit to him!"

The youth kissed her gently and held her in his arms. They remained together, arms entwined and lips touching, for the rest of the night.

In the morning the boy promised to defend the maiden against her unwelcome suitor and readied himself for battle. Blanche Fleur warned him against fighting so dangerous an enemy, but secretly she prayed that the young knight would defend her and win peace for her lands.

With the prayers of the townspeople rising to Heaven behind him, the youth rode through the gate to meet Anguiguerron. The cruel knight was camped outside with his men, certain that the town would surrender before nightfall.

"Young man, who sends you here?" shouted Anguiguerron.

The boy replied, "Why are you here and why have you been slaying knights and destroying this town?"

"This place must surrender today!" Anguiguerron demanded. "Blanche Fleur and her possessions must become the lawful property of my lord."

"Your words mean nothing to me!" cried the youth. "Give up all claim to this noble lady!"

"No!" Anguiguerron shouted back.

At this the boy pushed his toes into his stirrups, crouched forward, lowered his lance, and charged straight at Anguiguerron. They cracked their shields and splintered their lances. They hacked at each other with their swords until the boy knocked Anguiguerron off his horse. Leaping from his own steed, the youth stood over the wounded knight, pointing his sword at his enemy's heart. The boy threatened to kill him, but Anguiguerron implored him to spare his life.

Then, remembering that the worthy gentleman Gornemant had advised him never to kill a knight who begged for mercy, the young man pointed to the gate and exclaimed, "I will send you to beg mercy of my lady back there."

"She would surely have me killed!"

"Then I will send you as a prisoner to her uncle, Gornemant of Gohort."

"I would fare no better there!"

"In that case you shall be granted safe passage to the court of King

Arthur, where you shall be taken prisoner. You will announce to the court that I will not return until I have avenged the lady whom Sir Kay injured!" exclaimed the boy.

"So it shall be. Thank you for my life," replied Anguiguerron, and he departed.

The victorious youth rode back to Blanche Fleur's castle. That evening, the young noblewoman covered the youth with such gentle kisses that the door to his heart was opened.

When Prince Clamadeu learned what had happened to his steward, he sent twenty knights to Beaurepaire. The youth led the townsmen through the gates, and they boldly fought the knights. That day many suffered the point of the youth's lance, and those who did not die in battle were taken prisoner.

Next, Clamadeu sent five hundred knights and a thousand soldiers. They forced their way through the town's main gate, but archers on top of the surrounding walls released a storm of arrows. Then they dropped the massive portcullis and it crushed many of the enemy soldiers. Those who remained inside were taken prisoner.

In a rage, Clamadeu sent a message that he would fight the youth in a private contest on the plain the next day. Blanche Fleur and the townspeople tried to talk the boy out of this deadly match, but he ignored their protests. "Not for any person or for any thing will I ever abandon combat!" he declared.

When it was time to do battle, the youth and Clamadeu rushed furiously at each other, their shields cracking and their lances shattering. Hurled from their horses, they fought on the ground with swords until the boy gained the upper hand and Clamadeu, flat on his back, begged for mercy. Once again the young knight agreed to spare Clamadeu's life if the prince would journey to King Arthur's court and surrender.

As the youth entered Beaurepaire in triumph, the church bells clanged, and people danced wildly in the streets. The young warrior was proclaimed a hero and the shining knight of the lovely Blanche Fleur.

Having gained the lady and her land as his own, the youth could have remained there, but once again he thought about his mother and how she had fallen at the bridge, and he wanted to go and find her. Blanche Fleur pressed him earnestly to stay, but the youth explained that he had to discover once and for all if his mother were alive or dead. Should he find her alive, he would bring her safely to Beaurepaire, where he would agree to govern the land. Should he find her dead, he would also return. So in either case he would come back.

The youth rode away, far into the countryside, with his lance in its rest, wearing all his red armor. Praying to God that he would find his mother, he rode further and further into the vast and lonely countryside. He lost all track of time and direction, meeting not a single soul in the wilderness. Here the atmosphere seemed to grow mysterious, as if he were somehow entering another kind of world. At last, he came to a rushing river, where he caught sight of two men bobbing up and down in a tiny boat. The older, a nobleman, fished, while the younger rowed vigorously. As the boat lurched near, the young knight waved to the men and shouted at the top of his voice, "Hey! Ho there! Is . . . there . . . any . . . way . . . to . . . cross . . . river?" Above the roar of the churning current the nobleman cried back. "Impossible! . . . River . . . very . . . deep . . . treacherous. No . . . bridge . . . many miles . . . no boat . . . only . . . little skiff . . . we ride in."

The youth then inquired where he might find safe lodging. Pointing with his one free hand, the fisher directed the boy to his own manor, located in a valley beyond the next hill. "Go . . . up there . . . through . . . rock . . . you will . . . see . . . it."

Waving good-bye to the boatmen, the boy urged his horse carefully through a sharp cleft in the stone summit and looked down onto a broad valley spread out before him. But to his surprise and distress, there was nothing there to see but the vast blue sky above and the endless dense forest below. "What kind of trickery is this?" he murmured to himself. His eyes scanned the valley again and again, but he could see no human habitation. Then, as if by accident, he spied the tip of a stone tower poking through the trees in the far distance.

Riding down the steep slope, the youth crossed the valley forest and at last saw a splendid, square, turreted castle with its drawbridge lowered. As the boy rode over the bridge, he was met by four pages who took his armor and horse and presented him with fresh red wool clothing. After the boy had bathed, changed, and rested, he was led into a great square hall. In the middle was a magnificent four-sided bronze hearth, with enough space around it that four hundred guests could gather there for dinner. A gray-haired nobleman reclined on a couch near the blazing fire. He wore a black sable cap with a silk band around the top. The youth recognized him as the fisherman he had seen that afternoon on the river.

The boy's host greeted him warmly and apologized for not rising because his legs would not support him. They enjoyed a friendly conversation, and the lord asked him many questions about his recent travels. While they were speaking of the boy's journey from Beaurepaire, a page entered the room carrying a magnificent sword. The page exclaimed, "This sword is made of the finest steel. It is a gift to you, my lord, from your beautiful niece with the golden hair. It is crafted in such a fashion that it cannot break except in a certain way known only to the man who crafted it. The lady wishes that this sword be given to a knight who can use it ably!"

The nobleman took the sword and presented it to the youth with these words: "The hilt is made of the finest gold and the scabbard of silk brocade from Venice. This weapon was destined for you." At once, the youth buckled on the sword and gripped the handle firmly with his hand.

ext, another page passed slowly through the room holding a shining lance. From time to time, a drop of blood appeared miraculously on the blade's tip and slid down the shaft. The awestruck boy wished to ask about this but recalled Gornemant's advice not to ask childish questions, and so remained silent.

Next, two squires entered slowly, carrying many flaming candles set in golden candlesticks. Behind them walked a richly attired maiden. She carried a magnificent cup made of pure gold, encrusted with the finest gems imaginable. From this vessel streamed so dazzling a light that the candles and the roaring hearth fire lost their glow, just as the moon and the stars fade in the glare of the morning sun. Next came a noble maiden carrying a silver carving platter. This procession, led by the page with the bleeding lance, walked in stately fashion through the hall and disappeared into a nearby chamber. Wide-eyed, the boy watched this superb display and longed to ask where they were going and whom they were serving with these precious vessels. But for good or bad, he held his tongue and remained silent, so as not to appear foolish.

Soon a fine dinner of venison and rare wines was served on an ivory board, supported by ebony trestles and covered by a rich damask cloth. During each course of the long and sumptuous banquet, the maiden with the dazzling cup appeared. She passed through the great hall to the other, mysterious chamber and then returned. But again, although curious, the youth held his tongue. After dinner, the servants set up a couch and bedding for him. The crippled host was carried away to his bedchamber and the other guests departed for the night.

Now alone, the youth lay down to sleep, thinking to ask the following morning about the radiant cup and whom it served.

⁂

AT DAYBREAK, the boy awoke and found himself still alone. He put on his red armor and walked over to the mysterious chamber of the night before. Finding the door locked, he banged loudly, but there was no reply. Turning this way and that, he heard only the dull echo of his boots on the flagstones. He wandered outside into the vacant courtyard and discovered that his horse, shield, and lance were waiting for him. Mounting in silence, he looked around. He could neither

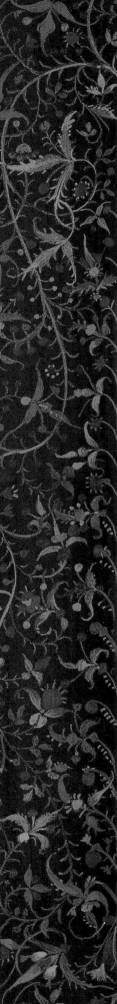

hear nor see anyone, but he noticed that the drawbridge was down. Quickly he urged his horse across it, expecting to find the castle's inhabitants hunting in the countryside.

He intended to ask about the bleeding lance and the marvelous cup, but just as he reached the other side of the bridge, his horse's hind feet abruptly lifted up. Glancing behind him, the boy was amazed to see the drawbridge rising, although he saw no attendant operating the device.

The youth had barely entered the forest before he encountered a maiden crying beneath an oak tree. "How miserable I am! I wish I were dead and with him, rather than alive and alone! Here I clasp the body of my dear lover, murdered by his enemy only yesterday," she moaned. The boy saw that on her lap she cradled the headless corpse of a knight.

"You and your horse do not look as if you have traveled far this morning," remarked the maiden through her tears, "and yet how could this be, as there is no lodging within many days' journey of this place?"

"I did indeed have lodging fit for a king," replied the youth, gesturing over his shoulder, "but a minute ago yonder."

"Then you must have stayed in the marvelous house of the rich Fisher King."

"I don't know if that is his name, but I saw him fishing on the river yesterday, and he agreed to give me lodging last night."

"While fighting in a war, he was wounded by a javelin in the thigh," said the maiden. "Painfully crippled, he can only fish, which is his greatest comfort. Tell me, did you see the bleeding lance?"

"Yes, I did," answered the boy.

"Did you ask why it bleeds?"

"No, I did not."

"That was bad of you! Did you see the fabulous cup?"

"Indeed, I did."

"And you saw from whence it came and to whence it traveled?"

"Yes, it was carried by a beautiful maiden. She was accompanied by pages carrying many candles. These were followed by a lady bearing a silver platter. They came into the hall and then passed to another chamber."

"Did you ask where they were going when they left the hall?"

"No, I said nothing at all."

"That is dreadful!" cried the maiden. "Please, what is your name?"

The boy did not know his name. But at that instant, for the first time in his life, he replied: "My name is Perceval the Welshman."

"No, your name is Wretched!" shouted the maiden. "Much suffering will come because you were afraid to ask about the cup and where it was being carried. If you had asked even one question, the Fisher King would have been healed, and he would have become strong enough to govern his land. Your silence was caused by your offense against your dear mother, who died of a broken heart because you deserted her. I attended her burial. You and I are first cousins, and I lived in your house when we were children."

Shocked and filled with grief, Perceval sank to his knees. Eager to hear more, he asked the maiden to accompany him, but she refused to leave her beloved knight until he was buried. Instead, she pointed toward the path her lover's killer had taken. Perceval vowed to serve the maiden by avenging her knight's death.

Perceval rode off and soon came upon another maiden. She sat upon a pony whose skin was stretched like thin parchment over its sharp bones. The maiden was filthy and pale, with deep circles under her eyes, and her frock hung in tatters around her ankles. Tears streamed down her face and soaked her parched skin. She told Perceval that she was the same maiden he had so rudely kissed and whose ring he had taken in the pavilion long ago. Ever since then, her knight had punished her by total neglect. The girl warned Perceval that if her knight returned, the angry man would kill him.

uddenly the maiden's knight burst upon them! Perceval confessed that he had kissed the maiden and taken her ring, but had not dishonored her in any other way. The enraged knight challenged Perceval. The two then charged at each other, splintering their lances and hacking viciously at one another with their swords. Perceval struck a violent blow to the knight's head so that, swaying from side to side, the knight slid from his horse and collapsed upon the ground. Perceval leapt from his steed and held his sword to the

knight's neck. As the knight cried out for mercy, Perceval again recalled Gornemant's warning. Rather than killing him, Perceval made the knight promise to take his lady to a nearby castle and give her rest and proper treatment. He must also provide her with clothing befitting her noble rank. When she was well enough, the knight was to take her to King Arthur's court. There he would surrender, revealing before all the court that it was Perceval the Welshman who had defeated him.

❧

PERCEVAL CONTINUED TO RIDE across the land in search of adventure. One morning, after a new snowfall, he happened into the neighborhood where Arthur's pavilions were now pitched. Looking toward the sky, he watched as a falcon struck a goose in flight. The goose shed three drops of blood from its injured neck as it fluttered to the ground. It soon struggled back into the air and flew away, leaving the white snow freshly stained by those scarlet beads. As Perceval stared intently, his thoughts turned to his lady, the exquisite Blanche Fleur, whose ivory cheeks were tinged with crimson. Falling into a deep trance, Perceval sat on his horse, as still as ice in the cold, breathless air.

The knights and ladies at Arthur's court observed the lone knight motionless on his horse and believed that he was asleep. Sagremore the Unruly put on his armor, mounted his horse, and rode out to invite Perceval to the camp. Perceval, still in a trance, did not respond. Growing impatient, Sagremore tried to provoke Perceval into a fight. Abruptly, Perceval shifted his gaze from the three drops of blood and swung his lance with such force that Sagremore tumbled to the ground. Then, fixing his gaze once more upon the drops of blood, Perceval continued his reverie of Blanche Fleur, while Sagremore limped back to Arthur's pavilions.

When Sir Kay, as cruel-hearted as ever, heard what had happened, he armed himself and went to find Perceval, hoping to bring him back by force. Perceval refused to accompany him and gave such a blow to Kay's chain mail that the man lurched backward over his charger's hindquarters and crashed down upon a rock. With a dislocated shoulder and broken arm, the miserable knight fainted and had to be carried back to camp, where the king ordered a skilled physician to attend to his wounds.

A wiser knight, Sir Gawain, rode out next and spoke more gently to Perceval. By this time, the sun had melted two of the three drops of blood on the snow, lessening Perceval's trance. Gawain's politeness and good humor won over the young knight. When Gawain explained that King Arthur himself had requested Perceval's presence, Perceval agreed to follow the other knight. They returned to King Arthur's pavilions, where Perceval was greeted by the king. Arthur learned that Perceval was the youth who had sent so many defeated knights back to his court, and he was greatly pleased. "If we have our way, you shall never leave this court again," Arthur declared.

Perceval greeted the queen and then the maiden who had smiled so joyously when he first visited Arthur's court. He promised to serve the young woman in any way that he could.

Thus the entire court was delighted at the return of Perceval the Welshman, and a great celebration was held. The court fool was very happy, too, because his prophecy about the greatest knight and the laughing maiden had come true.

On the third day of their celebration, an ugly hag perched on a mule rode into the middle of the great hall. She had a dirty neck and messy hair, and she carried a whip in her hand. Her eyes were like those of a rat. She had the nose of a monkey, the ears of a cow, the beard of a goat, and grimy, yellow teeth. Her back was crooked like a snake, her legs twisted, and in the middle of her chest there was a huge, disgusting hump.

This hideous creature greeted the king and the knights and then stared directly at Perceval, pointing her finger at him: "You stupid fool! When you were at the Fisher King's castle, why for God's sake didn't you ask about the bleeding lance and the marvelous bowl? Why didn't you say something? You were right there with the suffering Fisher King, and you were silent. You saw that the cup was carried to serve someone, but you buttoned your lips, wretch! If you had only asked, the king would have been healed. But now, you silly dunce, your lack of curiosity will cause many a nobleman and maiden to suffer, lands will be invaded, and cities devastated. Calamities will come and thousands will die, all because of you!" With these words, the repulsive woman spurred her mule and rode away.

Perceval was filled with shame. But there rose in his heart a firm determination. He solemnly vowed that until he found the miraculous lance and understood why it bled, he would never sleep in the same place two nights in a row. He would not cease to fight and to quest with all his heart and strength until he had learned who was served from the dazzling cup.

FIVE LONG YEARS PASSED, and a great forgetfulness came over Perceval. He wandered from place to place, never sleeping in the same spot twice. But as he journeyed, he forgot all about God. Five times spring came and turned to summer. Yet Perceval—though he defeated thousands of knights and sent them back to King Arthur's court—never thought to visit a church to observe Lent or celebrate Easter.

One day Perceval was riding through the forest when he came upon a group of knights and ladies walking barefoot and wearing coarse woolen garments. When they saw Perceval, they shouted, "Why are you riding in your armor like this on such a holy day, when all Christians should confess their sins?"

"What day is this?" asked Perceval.

"Indeed, it is Good Friday, the day of Our Savior's death on the cross," one of the ladies answered. "Don't you have faith in God and want to confess your sins?"

Astounded to hear this, Perceval replied, "Indeed I do." Then they told him that there was a chapel nearby where he could confess to a holy hermit.

Perceval made his way to the priest and told him the story of his life and his sin against his mother. He ended his tale by admitting that he had not asked about the miraculous cup or about the bleeding lance.

"Misfortune has come to you not because of your actions alone, but because you had no idea of what you did!" said the kindly monk. "You tore yourself from your mother so brutally that it never entered your mind she would die of shock and grief from losing you, you who were her only joy and happiness. Because you worshiped knighthood, craved combat, and longed to serve fair damsels far more than you loved God, you took Gornemant's advice much too strictly, stifling your curiosity, rather than learning when to use it. Thus, you neglected to ask vital questions regarding the marvelous events that occurred in the great Castle of the Fisher King. It was sin that held your tongue, because you wished to appear grown up and smart in the eyes of the world.

"But the Holy Scriptures teach us that if we think of ourselves as wise, we must first learn to be fools before we can really be wise. And Our Lord, when He was still on Earth, taught us that unless we become children again, we cannot enter the Kingdom of Heaven. You were too proud to ask about the bleeding lance and the miraculous cup, fearing you would look childish and foolish. Yet it was the healing Wisdom of God that was urging you to serve Him by becoming His clever fool and to have the courage to ask questions, so that the Fisher King could be cured by your own curiosity. There was a hidden monarch in the mysterious chamber who was served from the cup. He is my brother and the father of the Fisher King. Our sister was your mother. So you see, I am your uncle. That secluded monarch, now invisible to the world, is the Grail King. He lives by the holy Bread of Heaven carried in that wondrous cup. He requires nothing else to sustain him."

erceval was deeply moved by these words and fell into a profound silence. Then, smiling through his tears, he confessed all his sins, from beginning to end, and afterward remained with his pious uncle for two more days. On Sunday, the third day, it was Easter, the holiest day of the year. On this joyous occasion Perceval received Holy Communion with a clean heart and a quiet mind.

HERE, THE TALE OF PERCEVAL AND THE GRAIL as told by the medieval poet Chrétien de Troyes, comes to an abrupt end. Although Chrétien continues his narration with episodes involving the adventures of Sir Gawain, we hear not a word more about the greatest knight in the history of the world and of his further search for the Grail. Some people believe that Chrétien died before he could return to the chapters about Perceval and fully complete his story. It has also been said that, for some more mysterious reason, this legend—which is the tale of us all—has not yet been finished in the inner landscape of our hearts and minds.

But others, who lived during the generations following Chrétien, did finish the story of the Grail in various versions. Some tell of Perceval leaving the holy hermit and wandering for many years, eventually finding his way back to the Castle of the Fisher King, a place not found on any map and not reached by any road. There, full of the courage of God, he solemnly pronounced the question, "Whom does the Grail serve?" Instantly the Fisher King was healed, and with a blissful heart, the tired old man, who had suffered so long, passed to the joy of God in Heaven. Lands that had lain barren for years suddenly turned green with lush new growth. Flowers bloomed everywhere in place of thorns. Springs that were dry now gushed with the clear water of life. Sick animals were strong again. Poor people had food and money. Ugly maidens became beautiful, and old knights young and hardy once more. Peace descended upon all the kingdoms of Europe.

Ever after, the miraculous golden vessel remained in the custody of the greatest master of chivalry who ever lived, now known far and wide as Sir Perceval, the Wise Fool and the Grand Knight of the Holy Grail.

I like to imagine my own further conclusion to this tale. I see the fair and noble Blanche Fleur, she of the laughing gray eyes, of the ivory cheeks blushed with crimson, of the high clear forehead and the flowing golden hair. This courteous damsel comes to meet Perceval in the mysterious Castle of the Fisher King, where they are solemnly married in the Presence of the most Holy Grail. In this haven not shown on any map, that Interior Castle of our hearts and minds that is nowhere and yet everywhere, I see the young couple full of joy together, in purity and truth, dedicating themselves to the protection and adoration of that Sacred Cup, from which streams the life of the world.

May God be praised!

AUTHOR'S NOTE

In medieval times, a *romance* meant a story written in the ordinary language of the people rather than in Latin. Chrétien de Troyes, considered the greatest of the authors of courtly romance, wrote the earliest known version of the Perceval story. His tale in French, entitled *Le Conte du Graal* or *The Story of the Grail*, was instantly followed by continuations, also in French, including those by Wauchier de Denain, Gerbert de Montreuil, Mannesier, and Robert de Boron. Wolfram von Eschenbach wrote his own German version, *Parzival*, which was later used by Richard Wagner for his famous opera. Finally, in fifteenth-century England, Sir Thomas Malory composed his rendition entitled *Le Morte D'Arthur* or *The Death of Arthur*.

Not much is known about Chrétien. He was probably born near the French city of Troyes, in Champagne, about eighty miles southeast of Paris. Chrétien became the court poet of Marie, Countess of Champagne (daughter of Eleanor of Aquitaine and sister of Richard the Lionhearted) and later of Philip, Count of Flanders. It was during his last days of service to Philip, sometime around 1190, that Chrétien wrote *The Story of the Grail*, which he left mysteriously unfinished. The manuscript ends in mid-sentence. That may account for several loose ends in the tale, themes that are introduced but never resolved. Because the final section is primarily concerned with Sir Gawain and says nothing more about Perceval and the Grail, I have left it out of my retelling.

The exciting Celtic folktales of Ireland, Wales, and Cornwall were major background sources for elements of Chrétien's story. King Arthur himself really existed as an early British chieftain, but practically nothing historically is known about him.

Chrétien was more interested in showing a person's inner development from childhood to adulthood than he was in reciting endless episodes of medieval warfare. Chrétien depicts three stages in the adventure of his hero. The first is childish enthusiasm in a fool's paradise. The second is becoming an educated and sensible grown-up, which brings with it the death of imagination and the disenchantment of the world. The third fully mature stage is the return of awe and rapture, bringing a new enlightened innocence in which Heaven and Earth are united.

Young Perceval turns boldly away from his mother in order to become a gentleman knight. He is extremely lucky and successful, but his knightly pursuits can only take him so far. Blocked by a treacherous river he cannot cross, he is forced to enter a further stage of his education: learning the importance of spiritual things that lie beyond the technical skills and worldly behavior of knighthood. In time he stumbles into the mysterious Castle of the Grail, a condition of heart and mind, not an actual place on the map. Here, as a dinner guest in the splendid hall of the crippled Fisher King, Perceval sees a fabulous procession of young pages and maidens carrying precious vessels, including a magnificent cup (similar to a Communion cup or chalice) that dazzles so brightly that everything else pales by comparison. He has glimpsed the heavenly Source of Life and Wisdom, miraculously present here on Earth. Awestruck, he is too proud to ask about it, fearing to appear stupid. Because he has stifled his natural curiosity, the suffering of the ailing king and many others continues.

Later, after learning humility, Perceval painfully enters the third stage, which is that of a wise and much deeper simplicity. In some continuations of the tale, the young knight is granted a second visit to the castle of the Fisher King, where he finally asks the great question, "Whom does the grail serve?" At that instant, the ailing king is healed and the whole world is filled with glory.

As my professor, Joseph Campbell, once remarked, "Myth is not really about the meaning of life. Rather, it gives us the rapture of being alive."

May this rapture, the rapture of the wise fool, fill us all!

–John Perkins

PAINTER'S NOTE

Because *PERCEVAL: King Arthur's Knight of the Holy Grail* is a medieval tale, I decided to try an old technique used by medieval and Renaissance master painters from Europe and Russia. The Russian name for the technique is *levkas* and the western variant is referred to as *gesso*.

First, I took a specially prepared, cured wooden board that was about an inch thick and straight, since stretchers were set behind it to prevent warping. Then I glued a very light linen material to the board's surface. After it dried, I applied a layer of gesso. When the gesso dried, I polished the surface until it was perfectly smooth. Then I repeated the same procedure ten times—applying the gesso, waiting for it to dry, and polishing the board. Finally, the board was ready to be painted. Although gesso can "accept" oil paint or watercolors, I chose to paint with egg tempera.

Russian icons and masterpieces by medieval European and Renaissance artists are testimonials to the longevity of the gesso technique.

The book's designer, Michael Nelson, digitally reproduced different panels and details from the original painting to illustrate each chapter.

Gennady Spirin